I Won't Be *Sapphira*

ANNE GATES

ARCHWAY
PUBLISHING

Archway Publishing books may be ordered through booksellers or by contacting:

Archway Publishing
1663 Liberty Drive
Bloomington, IN 47403
www.archwaypublishing.com
1 (888) 242-5904

ISBN: 978-1-4808-2277-1 (sc)
ISBN: 978-1-4808-2278-8 (hc)
ISBN: 978-1-4808-2279-5 (e)

Library of Congress Control Number: 2015918190

Print information available on the last page.

Archway Publishing rev. date: 12/23/2015

To Albertha, Mom, Dad and My Inspiring Children

Contents

Introduction

The divorce was final. How did two born-again believers get to this point? Was it infidelity? Were there financial problems? Was there physical abuse?

Challenges and adversities are common forces within the family. In the United States, almost one in two marriages ends in divorce. Unfortunately, confessed Christians are among this statistic. Inclusive in that number are church leaders and pastors. Reasons for filing for divorce vary from one relationship to another, but in Kathy's case, *she refused to be Sapphira!*

The book of Acts in the Bible describes the history of the early Christian church in Jerusalem and records the accomplishments of the apostles as they were empowered by the Holy Spirit.

One of the practices of the early church was communal sharing, which was voluntary among the people and practiced before and after Pentecost. The fifth chapter of Acts describes the actions of a married couple, Ananias and Sapphira, in regard to communal sharing. They had sold their land for a certain amount of money and together decided to give the church a portion of their profit. However, when Ananias presented the offering to the church, he did so as if it were the *entire* profit.

"[He] kept back part of the price. ... Peter said, "Ananias, why hath Satan filled thine heart to lie to the Holy Ghost, and to keep back part of the price of the land? ... You have not lied unto men, but unto God" (Acts 5:2–4).

Hearing these words of conviction, Ananias fell down and died. Three hours later, his wife, Sapphira, not realizing her husband had died, appeared before Peter, who questioned her about the profit from their sold land. Sapphira repeated the same lie as Ananias. Consequently, she too fell to her death.

This biblical account is not typically a chapter of exposition in American churches, but three important words from this account pose as a point of emphasis: "three hours later." For approximately three hours, Sapphira was separated from her husband. Where was she? What was she doing that she didn't have knowledge of her husband's death? Was this divine intervention? If so, why?

God gave Sapphira time to make a decision regarding her salvation and her personal relationship with him. Would she follow her husband in a premeditated lie to the church or obey the principles of God?

Chapter 1

Mr. and Mrs. Washington

"Kathy, you look so beautiful."

"Oh, thank you, Mom," Kathy replied, distracted by the sound of footsteps overhead in the church sanctuary.

Kathy's mother, Mrs. Woodard, was applying the final touches to Kathy's makeup as they waited downstairs in their family church. Through the stained glass window, Kathy caught a glimpse of her future husband, pacing back and forth, giving directives to his groomsmen.

There wasn't a cloud in the sky, though it had rained two days earlier. *It's my wedding day, the most exciting day of my life,* Kathy thought. *In about one hour, I will become Mrs. Zacchaeus Washington.*

Zack, a Sunday school teacher and junior deacon, was tall, dark, and handsome. Kathy recalled watching him walk into the community store to purchase snacks on one of their dates. *How can a Sunday school teacher have such nice buttock?* she had thought. Though they had dated for nearly two years, Kathy and Zack had never played in the sheets. Now, Kathy smiled to herself. *Sheets, get ready. Tonight will be our night.*

The church sanctuary was filled to capacity. Ladies were dressed in their finest apparel, and the church mothers were wearing hats of various sizes and colors. Men were smiling, although some looked as though they were choking from their tight neckties.

Mendelssohn's "Wedding March" echoed throughout the church, and the huge mahogany church doors opened for the fourth time that year for a bride. The guests stood, looking eagerly toward the doors.

When Kathy and her father stepped into the church aisle, all eyes were on them. Seven bridesmaids and seven groomsmen stood poised and regal as they anticipated Kathy's entrance.

Kathy smiled and gently nodded in acknowledgment to her guests as she strolled down the fifty-foot aisle. Although her eyes honored her guests, her heart was fixed on her future husband.

The ceremony lasted for about an hour. Kathy wished that time could stand still on this glorious occasion. Then again, if time had been rendered motionless, she would have been deprived of her most exhilarating moment—Zack's and her first night of skin-blazing intimacy.

Chapter 2

Zacchaeus Washington was born in a small town in southern Georgia, the youngest of five children—three boys and two girls. His dad was a truck driver, and his mother worked in a clothing factory. His brothers handled most of the outdoor responsibilities while his sisters assisted their mother with household chores and often supervised Zack when their parents were away.

In elementary school, Zack was shy and respected his teachers, most of whom were females and quite strict. He was careful not to be the recipient of their "redirections."

In high school, Zack was still relatively quiet, but he loved to play sports, as he'd had a lot of practice playing football and basketball with his brothers. Classmates and teachers often praised Zack for his athletic performance, but no matter how intensely he practiced to improve his skills, the awards always went to another player. Joel, one of Zack's brothers, blamed "the system" for not recognizing the talent of its African American students.

One day, Zack's dad took him to a professional basketball game. Zack was so happy to experience this event with his father, but on the way to the stadium, Mr. Washington stopped at a white house with green shutters.

"Wait in the car, son," Mr. Washington said. About ten minutes later, he returned with a lady named Marian, who slid into the front seat.

Zack's heart beat fast, and his hands began to sweat as Marian's strong perfume filled the car. He was sure his dad could hear the angry pounding of his heart.

Mr. Washington smiled at Zack and said, "Son, are you ready?"

Zack replied softly, "Yes," but deep inside, he wanted to scream, "Hell, no!"

After that game, Zack never went with his dad to another event. And he never forgave his dad for cheating on his mother.

After graduating from high school, Zack attended a Division Two college, played basketball for one season, and then discontinued his participation in college sports.

Chapter 3

No Shining Knight

Old-school music played on the car stereo during Kathy's shopping spree with her girlfriends. Hip-hop was new, and many of their peers were riding the new wave, but Kathy and her friends still loved their R&B and gospel.

After five hours of visiting numerous shops and perusing interesting clothing and shoes, the ladies were ready to end their adventure. Kathy was now the proud owner of a new black-and-gray designer purse, and her friend Gigi had purchased a pair of black leather boots that she had admired for three weeks—with her wide feet, she was happy the store still had her size.

On their way home from the mall, Phyllis suddenly said, "Hey, Kathy, turn the radio down, I think I hear a scrubbing sound."

Kathy turned down the volume, and sure enough, she heard an awful noise. Frightened, Kathy didn't know what to do, but she felt confident that her new soul mate would come to their rescue. So she called Zack.

"Hi, honey. Something is wrong with the car. I keep hearing a loud scrubbing sound."

"It's probably your brakes," Zack said.

"Well, I've pulled over to the side of the road. I'm not too far from the house. Can you come help us?"

Zack paused for a moment before responding. "Kathy, I'm on my way to choir rehearsal. Just go to the nearest service station or auto-parts store. You probably just need brake fluid."

Kathy was totally dissatisfied with Zack's response. How could he refuse an opportunity to be her knight in shining armor and rescue her and her friends? Did he say choir rehearsal? He wasn't leading a song, and his choir wasn't singing for another three weeks. Besides, she didn't see a service station or auto parts store. Nevertheless, Kathy said, "Okay."

"Hey, girlfriend, we got this!" said Phyllis when Kathy related Zack's response. "There is a service station just around the next block."

A few minutes later, the problem was solved. An auto technician checked the car, and sure enough, the brake fluid was low.

Later, still disheartened by Zack's response, Kathy shared the account with her sister, Cindy.

"Forget it," Cindy advised. "You're being too sensitive."

Chapter 4

A Fallen Icon

"Hello?" Kathy whispered in a raspy voice, fumbling to turn on the light. She peered at the clock through half-open eyes. It was 2:38 a.m. *Early morning telephone calls always mean trouble,* she thought.

"Kathy," her sister said, "Mom has taken a turn for the worse. You need to get to the hospital right away."

Zack stirred beside Kathy. "What's wrong?" he asked.

"It's Mom. We need to go to the hospital."

Kathy's mother had been diagnosed with type 1 diabetes six years earlier. Within the past year, she had experienced complications with her kidneys, and fluid had accumulated in her legs and abdominal area. A kidney transplant wasn't an option, as she also had been diagnosed with hypertension.

Her mother's strength had been diminishing. One night when Kathy was visiting, she heard her mother trying to walk from her bedroom to the bathroom. Suddenly, there was a loud *thump* in the dimly lit hallway.

Kathy jumped off the sofa and ran to her mother, trying to lift her from the floor but failing miserably.

"Lord, please strengthen my arms," Kathy cried.

Kathy's brother hurried to the hallway to assist Kathy, and they carefully placed Mrs. Woodard in her bed, realizing that, regrettably, she would now need around-the-clock assistance.

Zack was moving slowly—he'd had a challenging and physically exhausting day at work, and now he'd been awakened in the middle of the night. Kathy took the wheel and drove to the hospital in silence. By the time they arrived, Mrs. Woodard had been pronounced dead. Lamentation and sorrow saturated the atmosphere of the room. Kathy's dad had died when Kathy was a young teenager. Now, she and her siblings were true orphans. Kathy felt physically ill.

"Our rock, our teacher, and the best cook in the world has transitioned to be with the Lord," she said, sobbing.

The funeral service was held three days later. Cindy coordinated most of the arrangements. The sisters wore white, and the brothers wore black and white. Many kind words of sympathy were expressed to the family. The siblings responded with appropriately traditional remarks, but their hearts were far removed from the present moment. They were remembering their mother …

Mrs. Woodard was a hard-working lady who dedicated her time and energy to her family. She worked at least six days a week, using the public transportation system until she could afford to purchase a car. Once a month, the entire family went to church together. On other Sundays, when she was working, she sent the children to their neighborhood church for Sunday school. In addition, Mrs. Woodard believed in having a clean house and a well-kept yard; to this philosophy, Kathy's mom and dad were glad to have five children.

Kathy believed that her mother was the best cook in the neighborhood. Many friends conveniently came to Kathy's house to play, especially on Sundays. They were usually rewarded with a great meal that often included fried chicken and a strawberry cobbler. Her mother always welcomed strangers and friends into their home. Mrs. Woodard's laughter and beautiful smile made anyone's woes seem better.

After the funeral service, Kathy and her siblings met at Cindy's house. Zack sat comfortably on the sofa, wrapped in his own thoughts. A few minutes passed, and then Zack rose from his seat and moved awkwardly toward his distressed wife.

"Kathy," he said, "I need to go to the church for just a moment. Kevin is speaking to our youth today, and I want to support him."

Kathy sat silently as she watched Zack exit the house. "Where is Zack going?" asked Cindy.

"Oh, he will be right back," Kathy replied.

Zack returned three hours later.

Chapter 5

Bon Voyage

The following year Zack presented Kathy with a wonderful surprise.

"Last year was a difficult year for you and your family," Zack told his wife. "Mother is truly missed. I want to do something special for you. We are going on a Caribbean cruise. Different scenery will help you rest and be restored."

Zack gently held Kathy in his arms as he went over the itinerary for their cruise. Kathy could see the twinkle in Zack's eyes as he described in great detail each day of the trip.

"Did you pack my favorite shirts," Zack asked when the day for their extravagant cruise finally arrived.

"Yes," Kathy assured him. "And I packed those black boxers I like to see you wear."

Zack chuckled.

The doorbell chimed—Cindy had arrived to drive

Kathy and Zack to the airport. Kathy couldn't believe Cindy was actually on time.

Punctuality was not Cindy's strength. Even her own wedding ceremony had been delayed for almost an hour. On the day of Cindy's wedding, she had decided at the last minute to go to the nail salon. The wedding planner was in panic mode, placing at least ten telephone calls, trying to locate Cindy. Meanwhile, at the church, the pianist played so many songs that the wedding guests thought they had had been invited to a concert. Finally, Cindy arrived. The wedding party was so glad to see her, they forgot about being upset about her tardiness.

Kathy and Zack's flight landed at Miami International Airport, and Zack flagged down a taxi to take them to the Miami port where they would board their cruise ship. They eagerly anticipated their first cruise together.

The cruise ship was huge, with a capacity of over two thousand passengers. The ship had multideck dining rooms, along with a casual buffet on the swimming pool deck. Many activities and entertainment shows for all age groups were featured on the week's agenda. Swimming, playing miniature golf, going to the movies, and visiting the bars were popular choices of entertainment for the passengers. Zack was excited and wanted to explore every inch of the ship, but on that first day, Kathy wasn't feeling so well. *Perhaps the excitement of making the trip is making my stomach a little queasy,* she thought. She encouraged Zack to explore while she took a nap.

Kathy had been asleep for about an hour when she heard Zack enter their cabin. Zack beamed with excitement as he told her about all the places he had visited on the cruise ship. He was most jubilant about meeting the captain of the ship near the bow. Zack could hardly wait to attend the Captain's Ball.

Kathy brought her favorite black-and-white evening dress for the occasion. It was a beautiful A-line, floor-length dress with a scooped neck and elbow-length lace sleeves. Kathy loved the way the dress emphasized her small waist. She pulled her hair back, away from her face, and made sure each strand was neatly in place. Kathy's seductive eyes and attractive smile were particularly appealing with her hairstyle.

Zack loves to see my hair in this style, Kathy reflected. *I'm sure to have his attention—and the attention of any other gentlemen who glance my way.*

Zack brought his black tuxedo with coordinating black-and-white vest and his black bow tie. The fit of his tuxedo was flawless! Of course, as far as Kathy was concerned, his broad shoulders and buttock were the main attraction.

When Kathy and Zack entered the dining hall, they were greeted and escorted to their table. Three other couples were seated at the table. They acknowledged each other with a smile and introduced themselves. Two of the couples had come on the cruise together and were well acquainted. Timothy and Elaine, the third couple, were about Zack and Kathy's age—perhaps a few years older. They were both somewhat short in stature. Elaine was from a small town in Georgia. Her large eyes, small nose, and big smile highlighted her face. As Elaine smiled and talked a lot, Timothy seemed to marvel at her every move. Elaine talked about her several brothers and sisters, who all shared Elaine's sense of social engagement—her "gift of gab." Zack and Kathy were glad to have Elaine at their table. She was humorous and kept their table well entertained with one story after another. Timothy constantly took pictures with his camera. If someone sneezed, Timothy took a picture.

Elaine was very interested in the dessert choices on the menu, especially the pastries and cakes.

"You know," Elaine said. "I learned to cook when I was in elementary school. I even baked cakes. One of my favorite cakes to bake was a peach cake, and one day, I had just removed a cake from the oven when my younger brother raced into the kitchen. 'Gimme that cake!' he shouted.

"At first, I just ignored him; but he exclaimed again, 'I told you to gimme that cake!' I looked at him and knew he was serious, because his fists were tightly clenched. I grabbed my cake and took off running toward the cornfields. My brother chased me. He was a fast runner, but, fortunately for me, I was faster. I finally reached the area of the cornfield where my parents were silting corn. Hiding in my mother's apron, I knew my cake and I were safe from the claws of my brother."

Everyone gasped during Elaine's story and then laughed. At first, everyone thought Elaine was exaggerating, but the expression on her face conveyed that her story was true.

The ship's captain circled the dining hall, stopping to visit with the guests at each table. When the captain reached Kathy and Zack's table, Zack was very excited, especially when the captain recalled their recent meeting on the bow. The captain then shared that he had been born in Rome and had been the master of his cruise vessel for over twelve years.

As the evening progressed, music filled the dining hall when the band began to play popular music from the '70s and '80s. Zack and Kathy danced all night. They were the center of attention when they waltzed to a popular love song of the '80s. Actually, they had planned their dance routine, and it was finely choreographed.

Before their cruise, Zack and Kathy had taken formal dance classes. Kathy had always loved to dance and to watch her parents dance. Zack, however, had two left feet. After much practice and determination, Zack became the favorite student of their class. Women would smile and request him as a partner for a least one dance. Zack beamed with delight. Kathy was so proud of him and not troubled by the other women's requests, because after all, he went home with her.

After the Captain's Ball, when Zack and Kathy returned to their room, Kathy again felt queasy, but this time she vomited. Zack tried to soothe Kathy, holding her close to him as they fell asleep.

Chapter 6

New Additions

*T*was Saturday morning at six twenty-three, and Zack was cautiously racing on the expressway to the hospital.

"Do you have my hospital bag?" Kathy asked.

"Yes, sweetheart," Zack answered.

At four o'clock that morning, Kathy had started having sharp pains in her abdominal area. She tried to relax and fall asleep, but fifteen minutes later, another pain would occur. Finally, the pains were coming ten minutes apart, and Kathy's lower back was aching intensely.

Her doctor, Dr. Patel, was ready to meet her at the hospital. Oh, remember the queasy feeling she was experiencing on their cruise? That was the beginning stage of her pregnancy.

Upon arriving safely at Johnson Memorial Hospital, Kathy was prepped for childbirth. She was excited and yet nervous. Even after reading several books, going to childbirth classes, and having many conversations with friends and relatives about their first pregnancies, she still felt anxious

"Kathy, you are going to be just fine," Dr. Patel assured her. "Now, let's see how much you have dilated. Five centimeters—we're almost ready."

It's funny how Dr. Patel says "we" when it's really me, Kathy thought.

Five hours and three additional cervical checks later, Kathy's water broke, and the medical team rushed into her delivery room. After ten minutes, the beautiful sound of new life filled the delivery room—twice. Their twins were welcomed into the world with bright lights and warm blankets. Zack stood tall and looked proud as he stared lovingly at their newborns. He leaned forward, kissed Kathy, and said, "We did great." Kathy smiled.

Nurses went in and out of Kathy's hospital room throughout the night. After nursing Micah and Michelle, Kathy was finally able to rest for a few hours. The next morning, Zack went to church.

After church, Gigi and Phyllis came to the hospital.

"Hello, Mother," Phyllis said. "Where are your beautiful babies?" She walked toward the hospital bassinet. "Sometimes it's hard to tell who or what newborns look like."

"I know you aren't talking about my babies," Kathy said with a chuckle.

"Kathy who are you expecting to visit you today?"

Gigi asked. "You just had two babies, and you are lying in bed with lipstick on."

They all laughed. Kathy rarely went anywhere without wearing lipstick. Gigi walked to the bassinet to look at the twins, and Phyllis sat in a chair close to Kathy.

"Girlfriend, Zack was at church today, walking around like a proud peacock," Phyllis said. "He was smiling, giving the guys bubblegum cigars, and slapping high-fives. Your sister was fussing at him about leaving you alone at the hospital. She told him to make a beeline back here. He just smiled and gave her a big hug. She laughed and pointed her finger toward the church exit door."

"Hello, sweetheart," Zack interrupted as he entered the room. "I hope your girlfriends aren't giving you a hard time. Let me know if I need to lay my hands on them." They all laughed again.

What a glorious day, Kathy marveled to herself. *I have a wonderful husband, a son and a daughter, close friends, delightful siblings, and a heavenly Father who orchestrated it all.*

Chapter 7

A Double Loss

The following year, tragedy knocked on the Washingtons' door again. It was two o'clock in the afternoon; the twins were having their midday nap. The ringing of the telephone interrupted Kathy and Zack's quiet home. Zack answered the telephone; his brother Joel was on the line.

"Hey, bro," Joel said. "I just received a call from Mom." He paused a moment and then said, "Dad just died."

"How is Mom?" Zack inquired.

"She's okay," Joel replied, "but we need to head home."

Zack's father had been ill for about two months. During that time, Zack never visited him. He still harbored angry feelings towards Mr. Washington due to unfavorable childhood events.

Mr. Washington was a very likable man to his neighbors and friends. He was also a great conversationalist who always greeted Kathy with a smile and a joke. The street news, however, was that Mr. Washington had children outside of his marriage. Zack would periodically comment to Kathy that he didn't want to be like his dad. Kathy often wondered how Zack, who wanted to be a church leader, could talk to others about God's forgiveness but could not extend forgiveness to his dad.

"Kathy, Dad just died," Zack announced as he hung up the phone. "Joel, his wife, and I are driving home tomorrow."

"I am so sorry, honey," Kathy said. "I'll join you in two days."

"Kathy, sweetheart, you don't have to come to the funeral."

"Excuse me? I don't have to come to the funeral?" Kathy exclaimed.

"You need to stay home with the babies. They need you," Zack insisted.

The next morning Zack, Joel, and his wife drove home to support Mama Washington. After their car turned the corner away from Zack and Kathy's house, Kathy immediately called her girlfriends, Gigi and Phyllis. A conference call was definitely in order.

"Zack doesn't want me to attend his dad's funeral," Kathy told her friends. "He said I needed to stay home with our children."

"He *what*?" exclaimed Phyllis. "Has he lost his mind?"

"Are you sure you heard him correctly?" added Gigi.

"Yes, Gigi, I am sure," Kathy answered.

Phyllis took control of the conversation. "Listen, when you learn the funeral date, you need to make plans to attend that funeral. We will rent a car, and I'll travel with you. Zack's family will find your absence very strange."

"Did Joel's wife go with him?" asked Gigi.

"Yes," Kathy responded.

"I will babysit the twins for you," Gigi said. "That is not a problem."

Four days later, Mr. James Washington's funeral was held. Phyllis and Kathy arrived two hours before the service.

"Hi, Mom," Kathy greeted Zack's mother.

"Hello, baby. I am so glad to see you. Zack told me you weren't coming because the twins were ill."

"I'm here, Mom. This is my friend Phyllis. She came with me."

Zack saw Kathy and came over to greet her. "Hey, baby. I am glad you're here."

Phyllis and Kathy smiled.

"Zack, Kathy, come here." Mom motioned to them. "I want you to meet my cousin Marian."

As Zack approached Marian, he realized this was the same woman his dad had taken to the professional basketball game all those years ago.

"You might remember that Marian went to that last basketball game you attended with Dad," Mom said. "I was supposed to go, but my legs were extremely sore that day. Marian used to play high school basketball, so I asked your dad to take her in my place."

Zack greeted Marian with a sigh of relief. For almost ten years, Zack had held a grudge against his dad because he thought Marian was his dad's mistress.

The next day, after returning home from the funeral, Kathy developed a migraine headache.

Chapter 8

A Personal Decision

Kathy! Kathy! Open the door!" Pepper simultaneously knocked furiously on the front door and rang the doorbell. Zack had left to run an errand, so Kathy ran to answer the door. There stood Kathy's twenty-year-old cousin Pepper, her face wreathed in a big smile.

Pepper occasionally babysat for Zack and Kathy, although Kathy suspected the young woman spent more time watching television and eating snacks than engaging in the process of babysitting. Kathy always fed Micah and Michelle before leaving home and changed the toddlers' diapers upon her return. The twins usually slept or played in their playpen when Pepper came over.

"Kathy, look at my new car!" Pepper exclaimed. "Zack helped me get it!" Parked in the driveway was a brand–new blue Mazda.

Zack had pulled in the drive behind Pepper. As he walked toward the house, he explained to Kathy, "I just cosigned with Pepper. Her parents are having hard times with their finances and needed my support. Pepper made the down payment. Take a ride with her, sweetheart. I'll stay with the twins."

Pepper's face glowed with excitement and a sense of accomplishment.

"This is a stylish car, Pepper," Kathy said as they pulled away from the house. "It certainly has a smooth ride, and I like your stereo sound. Now, are you sure you can handle your payments?"

"Of course. That's not a problem."

Pepper carefully drove her new car around the neighborhood, stopping at each stop sign and signaling for each turn. The neighborhood was relatively quiet and consisted of traditional two-level and Spanish-style ranch homes. Bradford pear and crape myrtle trees lined the front lawns. Most homeowners were professionals and owned at least two cars.

Zack was tossing a big red ball in the yard with the twins when Pepper and Kathy returned from their ride.

"It's a beautiful day for a drive," Zack said. "Not a cloud in the sky."

Kathy and Zack waved good-bye to Pepper as she zoomed away in her car.

"Honey, I know we didn't discuss another possible debt," Zack offered before Kathy could say anything. "I guess I just got caught up in the moment and Pepper's excitement."

Kathy elbowed Zack in his side. Zack pretended he was hurt and hugged Kathy.

Six months later, Zack started receiving telephone calls from Pepper's bank. Pepper's car payments were two months past due, and the bank was harassing Zack for a car payment. Zack telephoned Pepper to discuss her delinquent payments.

"I'll catch up on the payments during my next pay period," Pepper said. "I promise."

Another month passed, and Zack received an e-mail and certified letter from the bank.

"Kathy, Pepper is your cousin," Zack pointed out. "I know I cosigned her car loan, but maybe you could try to reach her."

Kathy stared at Zack and then said, "I'll try."

It's funny how people don't include you in making in-dependent decisions but then want you to share in their negative consequences. I guess that's a part of being married, Kathy thought.

The car loan was now three months past due, and the bank intended to repossess the car. Zack relayed the bank's message to Pepper, who had refused to commu-nicate with the bank. Finally, the "repo man" tracked down the car and repossessed it. Pepper was furious.

When Kathy was a teenager, her mother frequently

told her, "Always save some money for a rainy day." Following her mom's advice, Kathy had put aside money in an emergency fund. Now, she gave the money to Zack to become current on the car payments and retrieve the car. Two months later, Zack sold the car. Eight hundred dollars were lost in the transaction. According to Zack, the whole situation was Pepper's fault.

Chapter 9

Church

Zack and Kathy became increasingly involved in church projects. Kathy worked with the missionary department, and Zack was now an ordained minister, overseeing the church's youth departments.

Young adults and children liked to be in Zack's presence; he was a true advocate for them. Zack admired the church pastor and aspired to follow in the pastor's footsteps. Whatever Pastor Emory Hill desired, Zack would try to fulfill his wishes.

Most of the church membership admired the Washington family, but there were a few members, especially women, who felt differently about Kathy. Kathy was not considered a "humble" sister of the church because she liked to ask questions.

Even as a child, Kathy had an inquisitive nature. *How else can you know something if you don't ask questions?* she'd thought. In school, class participation and oral discussions were Kathy's strengths, but now, in church, asking questions was somehow perceived as antagonistic behavior. The first time Kathy asked a question at a church annual conference, the room became completely silent. The atmosphere immediately became so tense that Kathy wondered what she had done wrong.

Kathy and Zack attended a small church with "doors that swung on welcome hinges." The church membership was primarily neighborhood families. Some of the established members were invested, but they never displayed a sense of arrogance or self-righteousness.

Lately, church membership had expanded outside the neighborhood and had grown tremendously. Several members drove more than twenty miles to attend service. There was a war in the Middle East, and everyone was gravitating to church. Families were seeking God and his salvation.

Pastor Hill taught and preached the unadulterated Word of God. Each sermon was sprinkled with one of Pastor's "Christian jokes." People always laughed, even if the jokes were repeats. Pastor Hill served as a leader, pastor, teacher, and preacher. It was not uncommon to find him and his wife making frequent hospital and prison visits.

The mature ladies and mothers of Gentle Springs Baptist Church were very kind-hearted and great mentors. They were known for the beautiful, fancy hats they all wore, especially on first Sundays. On this particular

Sunday, Sister Bing was wearing a new hat—a huge purple chapeau shaped like a sombrero. She stood in front of Kathy, beaming, waiting for a reaction.

"Oh my, Sister Bing! I love the color of your new hat," Kathy said. Sister Bing smiled and went to another member, hoping to receive more words of admiration.

The following week, the church would celebrate its twenty-fifth anniversary. Everyone was excited.

"This is going to be our best church anniversary!" exclaimed Sister Bing. Of course, Sister Bing made that declaration every year. "What are our colors?" she asked.

Kathy smiled and answered, "Royal blue and silver."

Sister Victoria Stapler, one of the church leaders, was the chairperson for the church anniversary. Although Sister Stapler only recently had joined Gentle Springs, she was bossy and demanding. Church gossip was that Sister Stapler made large monetary contributions each month and thus had been elevated to a position of importance in the church.

Sister Stapler believed the whole world revolved around her and most people responded to her commands. Kathy was not impressed or intimidated. Zack, however, believed Sister Stapler's influence would help him become a pastor one day.

Regardless of anyone's opinion, Sister Stapler beamed with excitement as she stamped around the church, planning for Gentle Springs's big event.

Ministers and their wives had been assigned to serve as facilitators for different activities throughout the week.

"Zack, what are our assignments this year?" Kathy asked. Zack did not respond. "Zack? Honey? What are we doing together this year?"

Zack smiled weakly. "I have been asked to serve as the master of ceremonies for our Tuesday evening event."

"You mean both of us, don't you?"

"No, Sister Stapler just asked me to do it."

The next day Kathy checked the ministers-and-wives weekly assignments. All ministers and their spouses were given joint assignments—except Zack and Kathy. When Kathy brought this to Zack's attention, he simply shrugged.

Sister Stapler and her "sister clique" often found subtle ways to glorify Zack but belittle Kathy and Zack's marriage.

Tuesday evening arrived, and most pews were filled to capacity. Kathy had purchased a pin-striped blue suit for Zack. His fashion-model body wore any suit very well. Kathy, Micah, and Michelle sat near the front of the church to encourage Zack and embrace his words. Their clothing was coordinated with Zack's colors.

After honoring God and Pastor Hill, Zack acknowledged Sister Stapler and his brother, who was in attendance. Elaine, who recently had moved to the city, nudged Kathy in her side.

After the service, Zack and Sister Stapler received many generous remarks from the congregation members.

Gigi approached Kathy. "Girlfriend, you really dressed Zack and the twins tonight. Zack looks like a Hollywood star—I almost thought he was related to Denzel or Kevin."

Kathy laughed.

"I also liked the way you continued to smile and look confident, even when Zack failed to acknowledge his family," Elaine added.

"Well," Kathy replied, "I admit I was pinched a little, but only what we do for Christ will last. Besides," Kathy added with a thin smile, "anyone can forget."

Zack and Kathy continued to embrace church responsibilities and move closer in their relationship to Christ. Each month, Pastor Hill allowed one of his ministers to present a sermon. From the pulpit, Zack preached with confidence and passion about his love for his children and his wife. Women would embrace his words with awe and admiration. At home, however, a different Zachary existed; at home, pride and deception began to raise their ugly heads.

Chapter 10

"Michelle, please place the butter back in the refrigerator," Kathy reminded her daughter.

"Yes, Mom," replied Michelle as she wiped the residue of orange juice from her upper lip.

Saturday mornings were always a favorite breakfast day. Kathy generally put on a performance when she served the family's favorite, pancakes. When the children were younger, green eggs often accompanied the main course.

"Hey, Mom, May I please have more French toast?" yelled Micah.

"Of course, Micah, and you know you don't have to yell to make your request," answered Kathy.

"That's right," Michelle and Zack responded in unison.

Later, Kathy gathered her purse and keys and headed toward her car. "Dog," she said with a sigh. "I guess I have to take my car to the car wash again."

Zack used to take pride in hand-washing and maintaining the cars on Fridays, his day off work, but now that seemed to be a thing of the past. Kathy waved good-bye to Zack as he stood at the garage door with a toothpick in his mouth.

The parking lot of the grocery store was crowded with dozens of cars, as Kathy had expected. Kathy noticed a car exiting its space and hurried to occupy the spot. "Thank you, Jesus," she said.

As Kathy got out of her vehicle, she noticed John, one of her fellow church members, exiting his new car.

"Hello, John. That's a sharp car you have," she said with a smile. John did not respond. *Maybe he didn't hear me*, Kathy thought.

Kathy pulled out her shopping list and began to walk the store aisles. The grocery list was much longer now than when the twins were babies. Kathy made a concerted effort to purchase at least a few favorite items for each family member, but broccoli would always remain on the list, whether they liked it or not. As Kathy marked another item off her list, she heard a familiar voice call from behind her.

"Sister Kathy."

She turned and saw John again. "Oh, hi. How are you, John? I tried to get your attention in the parking lot."

"I know," replied John, lowering his head. "Actually, I was trying not to speak to you."

Kathy's mouth dropped open, but she stood silently.

"Well, you see," John continued, "I am really upset with your husband. My wife and I have been arguing a lot lately, so I invited Minister Washington to our home to counsel us. Well, he counseled us all right; he told my wife to divorce me. Now, I know I hang out with the guys and drink occasionally, but I love my wife and my son. I thought Minister Washington was going to focus on reconciliation, God's love for families, and the importance of keeping our marital vows. But he was biased throughout the entire consultation. After he left, I tried to refer my wife to the scriptures in 1 Corinthians 7:10, which encourages married couples to stay together. My wife just said, 'Minister Washington didn't talk about that scripture.' I should have kicked your husband's ass out of my house." He shook his head. "I'm sorry, Sister Kathy. I have to go."

Seconds passed, but Kathy didn't move; she remained standing in the same spot with her mouth agape. Kathy was aware of Zack's bias toward a younger couple of the church, but she was totally caught off guard when she learned of his pro-divorce philosophy. Kathy tried to focus on her grocery list but was too distraught over what she'd learned about John and his wife.

When Kathy arrived home, Michelle and Micah

raced to the car to retrieve the grocery bags. Zack was mowing the lawn. His sweaty T-shirt outlined his small bulging stomach as he walked toward the car.

"Give me some sugar," he said, with drops of salty sweat falling down his face.

Kathy laughed. "I saw Brother John at the grocery store," she said.

"That brother can really grill chicken," Zack answered.

"He told me about your counseling session with him and his wife," Kathy added.

Zack did not respond.

After placing the groceries in the pantry and refrigerator, Kathy telephoned Gigi.

"What's up, girlfriend?" Gigi asked.

"Gigi, today I saw Brother John Patton in the grocery store. He was …"

"Oh. Have he and his wife separated yet?" asked Gigi.

"How did you know about him and his wife?" Kathy asked.

"Girlfriend, you really don't hear a lot, do you? Our pastor's niece tells just about everything that happens in Pastor's house. So I guess you also don't know that according to reliable sources, Zack told John's wife to divorce him."

"I didn't," replied Kathy, "but I do now. John told

me himself." She sighed heavily into the phone receiver. "Before Zack and I married, we both declared that we did not believe in divorce."

"Well, girlfriend, I guess he has changed his mind," declared Gigi.

Chapter 11

Favoritism

The squeaking sounds of the garage doors welcomed Kathy home from another long day at work. She rested in her car for about two minutes before entering the house. As soon as she opened the kitchen door, Michelle rushed down the steps to greet her.

"Mommy! Mommy!" she cried. "Daddy choked me!"

Kathy looked at Michelle's red eyes. It appeared as though she had been crying for a long time.

"It is Micah's time to wash dishes," Michelle went on. "Daddy wouldn't listen to me when I told him. I got mad, and then Daddy got mad, and he choked me." She broke into sobs. "I told you Daddy likes Micah better than me!"

This particular theme of favoritism had visited the Washingtons' household on several occasions. At times, it was very obvious. On the twins' tenth birthday, Zack and Kathy decided to give each twin a color television. Zack selected the sets and brought them into the house for the big birthday surprise. Micah received a nine-teen-inch screen, and Michelle received a thirteen-inch screen. Micah was ecstatic, and Michelle smiled and thanked her parents. As Zack and Kathy prepared for bed, Kathy asked him about the size differences of the television screens. Zack explained that Micah needed a larger set to play video games. "Besides," he said, "both sets are made by the same company."

Now, Kathy comforted Michelle and listened to the words of her broken heart. "Daddy choked me," Michelle repeating, laying her head on Kathy's lap. Kathy gently stroked her daughter's hair until Michelle fell asleep.

Kathy's legs felt limp as she walked lifelessly upstairs to the second level of the house.

Micah was in his bedroom. "Mommy, I tried to tell Dad," he said quietly. "Dad just said he told Michelle to clean the kitchen."

Kathy entered their bedroom. Zack was sitting at his desk, reading his Bible.

"What happened?" Kathy asked.

Zack lifted his head and looked at Kathy. "I told Michelle to clean the kitchen. And you're supposed to be on my side," he said.

Kathy stared at Zack and asked, "What scriptures support physical abuse? We suppose to discipline our children, not choke them." Kathy walked out of the bedroom door, closing the door behind her, and went to the guest bedroom. Throughout the night she prayed and cried to God. She wept deep inside her soul for her husband and her children. Emotionally and spiritually, she felt torn. The world says, "Stand by your man." God's word teaches his followers to "Honor him with their lips, heart and service." The man Kathy and her children knew at home was quite different from the man who spoke from the pulpit.

The next day, Michelle accompanied Kathy to the grocery store. On the way there, they talked about child abuse and God's word regarding the role of parents and children within the family.

"Mommy, do you think Dad is abusive?" Michelle asked. "I should have just obeyed him, but he should have listened to me too. I know he loves me, but he better not put his hands on me again."

Michelle chose to wait in the car while Kathy went in the grocery store. An admirer who had been watching Kathy approached her and asked for her telephone number. For the first time in her marriage, Kathy almost complied.

For the next two days, the house was very quiet. Kathy spent quality time with Michelle and Micah. On the third day, Zack purchased a nineteen-inch color television for Michelle. Michelle was excited but really just wanted an apology and her father's love.

The following week, Zack did not go to work for two

days. Kathy inquired about the abrupt change in his routine—Zack rarely missed work; it was hard to keep him
home, even when he didn't feel well. Reluctantly, he told
Kathy he'd been sent home because he'd violated one of
his company's policies. Kathy realized she was watching
a man—a minister, whose ultimate desire was to please
God—change.

Kathy had another migraine headache.

Chapter 12

Where Is the Money?

Zack was a person of few words. When there was an issue of concern, he denied the existence of the issue or just remarked, "I am handling it."

As Kathy reflected on Zack's abusive behavior with Michelle, she wondered if he was transferring financial frustrations to Michelle. He was mismanaging money in their joint bank account, and they'd received pink-colored statements from the mortgage company. When Kathy questioned Zack about insufficient funds, he only would give her another of his favorite responses: "I didn't think you needed to know."

One day Kathy received a telephone call from Zack's mother. Mrs. Washington was such a lovely, tall lady— dark, with beautiful, smooth skin. When she smiled, Kathy always felt that hopelessness transformed to hope. Even in Mrs. Washington's senior years, she enjoyed riding a bicycle, saying it was a pleasurable exercise for her.

On this day, she surprised Kathy by saying, "I'm

calling to thank you and Zack for my new air conditioner. I really appreciate the money you sent also."

"Oh … you are welcome, Mom," Kathy replied, even as she thought, *Now I know one of the reasons our mortgage wasn't paid on time.*

At the beginning of the new calendar year, Kathy collected the financial statements to file taxes. As she compiled the documents for filing, she realized that important statements were missing. Zack was in his office, preparing a sermon for Sunday's worship.

"Zack," Kathy called to him. "I can't find your documents for our taxes."

Zack emerged from his office. "I have already filed my taxes."

"What do you mean you have already filed your taxes?" asked Kathy.

"I already filed." Zack said. "You're smart. You figure it out." Zack returned to his office.

Kathy searched the file cabinet where previously filed tax returns were stored. She found Zack's current year tax return. Zack had claimed the twins, the mortgage interest on the house, and their property taxes as his deductions. Kathy was absolutely speechless and afraid for Zachary. *Truly*, she thought, *he has lost his mind!*

Kathy's eyes brimmed with tears as her mind filled with conflicting thoughts. She picked up her cell phone to call Zack's trusted minister friend.

"Minister Timothy," Kathy said, sobbing into the phone. "Zack and I need you. Please come quickly."

An hour later, Minister Timothy arrived.

"Thank you for coming," Kathy said as she wiped the tears from her face.

Timothy and his wife, Elaine, entered the house. Kathy explained the tax-filing situation to them.

"Where is Zack?" Timothy asked.

"He is in his office," answered Kathy.

Timothy left the women in the family room and went to Zack's office alone. He tapped gently on the paneled office door.

"Come in," Zack called out.

In the family room, Kathy twisted her hands nervously. "Something is terribly wrong, Elaine," she said. "I don't know how much more I can endure. It appears as though he wants me to be angry and frustrated with him. He leaves the house at least once a week to 'run errands.' When I question him, he tells me the errands are related to ministry work. I am having more and more migraine headaches."

"Well," Elaine said quietly, "in the big picture, Satan is always trying to destroy families and create confusion. I do know, however, that Pastor Hill was annoyed with some of the questions you asked last month at our church conference. Maybe he spoke to Zack about his feelings. Remember the questions you asked regarding the church's lack of support for outreach ministries?"

Kathy nodded. "Yes, I remember, but Zack had asked me to make the inquiries."

Footsteps in the hall announced the entrance of Minister Timothy and Zack. Minister Timothy prayed for Kathy and Zack. He petitioned God for marital unity and heavenly guidance. Kathy and Zack thanked Timothy and Elaine for their visit.

Zack gently held Kathy's hand as he waved good-bye to the couple, but when Timothy's vehicle disappeared around the street corner, he abruptly turned to Kathy and said, "My position regarding our tax returns remains the same."

On Sunday morning, Zack acknowledged his beautiful wife, Mrs. Kathy Washington, and his children in front of the congregation before he delivered his sermon. Zack made eye contact with Kathy, but he had an insolent smile on his face.

Kathy thought of the scripture passage from Samuel 16:7. "Man looks on the outward appearance, but the Lord looks on the heart."

At church, Zack continued to present his marriage with Kathy as a united, flawless union. *What responsibility do I have in this lie?* Kathy wondered. *Am I promoting a spirit of deception by my silence? Would God see me as another Sapphira?*

Chapter 13

A New Beginning

Chimes from the oak grandfather clock vibrated the stillness of the air. Another day of silence passed. Micah and Michelle visited with friends so they could be away from the house; when they were home, they spent more time in their bedrooms. Animosity hovered like a thick cloud over the Washingtons' household.

"Zack, we need counseling," said Kathy.

"I will make an appointment with Pastor Hill," Zack responded.

"We need to schedule counseling with a licensed marriage or pastoral counselor. Confidentiality needs to be honored."

"You just don't like Pastor Hill."

"What I don't like is hypocrisy," Kathy responded. "Pretending to operate in the character of Christ at church and living like a ... well, quite differently at home."

"You just want to put our business in the streets!"

Zack exclaimed, He walked away from Kathy and grabbed his keys. "I need to run some errands," Zack snapped, never looking at Kathy.

"I love you, Zack," Kathy called after him, "but I won't be Sapphira."

Over the next three nights, Kathy tossed and turned in her bed. Zack was now sleeping in their guest bedroom. Sharp pains pierced her stomach daily. Contemplating the idea of a legal separation brought despair to her spirit. Besides, Zack did not favor a separation.

"Let's just live in the house together but have separate lives," Zack suggested.

More deception, Kathy thought. She was hoping Zack would agree to and encourage repentance and family unity.

As Kathy reclined on the sofa one night, her heart and lips talked to Jesus. "But Father, Zack is a minister. Why are we going through this? What did I do wrong?"

Quietly, the Holy Spirit urged Kathy to go to the lower level of the house. As she wandered in the basement, Kathy found herself browsing aimlessly through storage boxes. Old, slightly mildewed objects filled the boxes. Suddenly, a blue envelope addressed to Zack caught her attention. She opened the envelope and took out the letter. As she read the fading print, the contents of the letter brought both liberation and sadness to her soul. A voice from Zack's past echoed from the pages of the letter. Lies and deception had existed before their marriage vows were ever spoken. A seed planted in Zack's past might one day knock on his door.

***

"Kathy, where are you?" Cindy asked into the phone.

"I'm in the parking lot."

Cindy sighed. "You have been in that parking lot for the past four days."

"I know," Kathy agreed absently. "Cindy, hold on for a minute, please."

Kathy tossed her cell phone in her purse, got out of the car, and walked toward the entrance to the building. One step, two steps, three steps … Kathy read the name etched on the glass pane: Tarsh and Bison Law Firm.

Kathy could hear Cindy yelling her name. She fished her phone out of her bag and said, "I hear you Cindy."

"What are you doing?"

When Kathy answered, her voice was filled with determination. "I just signed the appointment log."

The news of Zack and Kathy's marriage buzzed throughout the church. The impact of their separation was devastating and hurtful to many. Many who wanted to believe a flawless fairy-tale marriage blamed one spouse over the other. Close friends scattered, family members were disappointed and angry, and some were even punitive.

In the midst of the storm and public ridicule, Kathy found peace. Kathy's peace was in knowing that within her "approximately three hours," God's opinion of her was more important than man's viewpoint. Kathy made a personal decision to trust God's provision and guidance. She was willing to give up church popularity in order to avoid presenting a lie.

***

Ultimately, every Christian will be granted "approximately three hours" to make decisions that are in opposition to God's principles with regard to relationships with friends, family members, employers, coworkers, or church members. God's grace and mercy provide us with "a way of escape" and "forgiveness" (1 Corinthians 10:13; 1 John 1:9).

Making a deliberate decision to disobey God's word could lead to dire or irreversible consequences. Sapphira's premeditated decision to conspire with her husband led to her spiritual and physical death.

Made in the USA
Columbia, SC
23 June 2021